Red Robin
BOOKS
Where story matters

Red Robin Books is an imprint of Corner To Learn Limited

Published by
Corner To Learn Limited
Willow Cottage • 26 Purton Stoke
Swindon • Wiltshire SN5 4JF • UK

ISBN 978-1-905434-01-5

Original text © Neil Griffiths 1999
First published in the UK 1999
Reprinted 2002
New edition with revised text 2007
Illustrations © Judith Blake 2007

Design by
David Rose

Printed by
Tien Wah Press Pte. Ltd., Singapore

If Only ...

Neil Griffiths

Illustrated by Judith Blake

One afternoon in early summer, a tiny black caterpillar crept from beneath a leaf and felt the warmth of the sun brush against its back.

It crawled

towards a flower
bed bursting with
early summer flowers.
A tall red poppy had
caught its eye.

There, dozing in the middle, lay a **plump** white-tailed bumble bee. The caterpillar looked at its velvety coat of black and yellow and sighed,

"If only I had such a lovely stripy coat."

The bumble bee heard and grinned.

The caterpillar was then dazzled by sunlight that had caught the wings of a dragonfly hovering above a purple water iris.

"If only I had such shiny wings," it sighed.

The dragonfly peered below and chuckled.

Suddenly a meadow grasshopper leapt from behind a lupin flower and burst into song.

The caterpillar listened to the grasshopper's music-making.

"If only I could sing such a beautiful song," it sighed.

The grasshopper stopped singing and laughed.

Thinking the grasshopper was making fun of it, the caterpillar climbed to the top of a tall sunflower to hide.

higher ...

Higher and

... it climbed until it reached the large flower head. It was not alone. A two-spot ladybird had flown in, in search of juicy green aphids.

"If only I had such a polished red and black wing case," it whispered. The ladybird stared at the caterpillar and giggled.

The caterpillar began to feel a little *dizzy* and so it took a short cut to the garden below along a thin thread attached to a flower pot.

Lupin

Lavender

Nearing the end
of its *descent,*

the caterpillar suddenly froze
at the sight of a garden spider
busily finishing a new web.
   "If only I could weave such
a fine web," it sighed.
The spider paused in its work
and smiled.

In need of a rest, the caterpillar decided to sleep inside a flower pot. Feeling a little cold, it grew a new, tougher, outer skin to keep warm. There it slept for sixteen days.

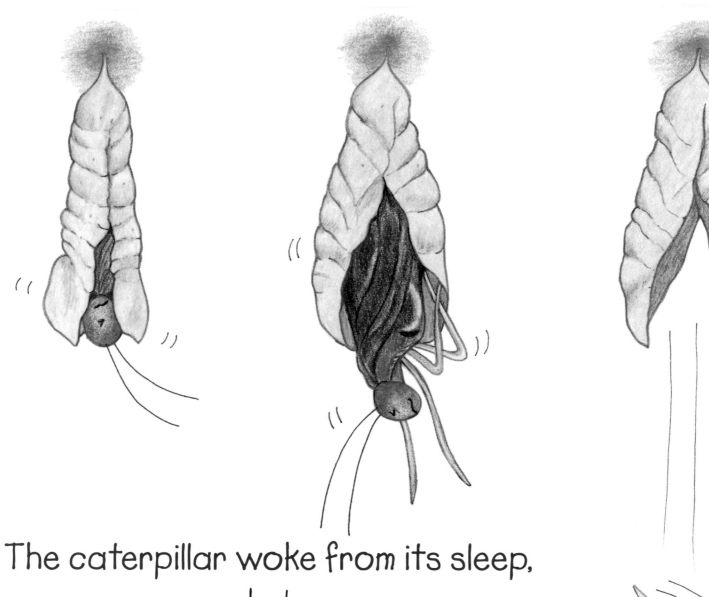

The caterpillar woke from its sleep, feeling very squashed in its new skin. It began to stretch and push and, after several hours, fell to the ground with a bump!

It c^r^{a}$_w$ $_l^{e}_d$ from the flower pot
and let the sun warm its crumpled body.

In the flower bed beyond,
tiny pairs of eyes were
watching and waiting.
One by one, each of the mini-
beasts came out of hiding.

The bee buzzed ...

the dragonfly danced ...

the grasshopper hopped ...

the ladybird fluttered ...

and the spider spun,

as they looked on in admiration.

"What are you looking at?"
asked the butterfly.

"You!" they replied together.

"Me?" asked the butterfly.

"Yes, you!" they replied.

"Why would anyone want to
look at me?" sighed the
butterfly sadly.

"Because you are a beautiful
butterfly," they all cried.

"A butterfly? But ..."

The butterfly took a closer look at itself and could hardly believe its eyes. It had turned into the most beautiful Peacock butterfly.

"You knew, didn't you?" said the butterfly excitedly.

"Yes, we knew!" replied the garden creatures.

"If only I had known too!" sighed the butterfly.